Cinderella

And Other Tales from Perrault

Cinderella

And Other Tales from Perrault

ILLUSTRATED BY

Michael Hague

Henry Holt and Company
NEW YORK

Published by Henry Holt and Company, Inc.,
115 West 18th Street, New York, New York 10011.
Published in Canada by Fitzhenry & Whiteside Limited,
195 Allstate Parkway, Markham, Ontario L3R 4T8.

Library of Congress Cataloging-in-Publication Data
Perrault, Charles, 1628–1703.
[Contes de fées. Selections. English]
Cinderella, and other tales from Perrault / illustrated by Michael
Hague.
Summary: An illustrated collection of Perrault fairy tales,
including "Cinderella," "The Sleeping Beauty," and "Blue Beard."
ISBN 0-8050-1004-1
1. Fairy tales—France. [1. Fairy tales. 2. Folklore—France.]
I. Hague, Michael, ill. II. Title.
PZ8.P426Cg 1989
398.21′0944—dc20   89-7626

Henry Holt books are available at special discounts
for bulk purchases for sales promotions, premiums,
fund-raising, or educational use. Special editions
or book excerpts can also be created to specification.

For details contact:

Special Sales Director, Henry Holt and Company, Inc.,
115 West 18th Street, New York, New York 10011

First Edition
Printed in the United States of America
1 3 5 7 9 10 8 6 4 2

Contents

The Sleeping Beauty

1

Little Red Riding Hood

13

Blue Beard

21

Master Cat, or Puss in Boots

29

The Fairies

39

Cinderella, or The Little Glass Slipper

45

Riquet with the Tuft

55

Tom Thumb

67

The Sleeping Beauty

There were once a King and Queen who were very unhappy at not having any children. Vows, pilgrimages, everything was tried, but nothing was of any avail; at length, however, a little daughter was born to them.

There was a splendid christening. For godmothers they gave the young Princess all the Fairies they could find in the country. They were seven in number. When the ceremony was over, all the company returned to the King's palace, where a great banquet had been prepared for the Fairies. The table was magnificently laid for them, and each had placed for her a massive gold case containing a spoon, a fork, and a knife of fine gold set with diamonds and rubies.

But as they were all taking their seats, there was seen to enter an old Fairy who had not been invited, for everyone thought that she was either dead or enchanted, as she had not been outside the tower in which she lived for upward of fifty years. The King ordered a cover to be laid for her, but there was no possibility of giving her a massive gold case such as the others had, because there had been only seven made expressly for the seven Fairies. The old Fairy thought she was treated with contempt, and muttered some threats between her teeth. One of the young Fairies, who chanced to be near her, overheard her grumblings and was afraid she might bestow some evil gift on the young Princess. Accordingly, as soon as they rose from table, she went and hid herself behind the hangings in order to be the last to speak and so enable herself to repair, as far as possible, any harm the old Fairy might do. Meanwhile the Fairies began bestowing their gifts on the Princess. The youngest, as her gift, promised that she should be the most beautiful person in the world; the next Fairy, that she should have the mind of an angel; the third, that every movement of hers should be full of grace; the fourth, that she should dance to perfection; the fifth, that she should sing like a nightingale; the sixth, that she should play on every kind of instrument in the most exquisite manner possible. It was now the turn of the old Fairy, and she said, while her head shook more with malice than with age, that the Princess should pierce her hand with a spindle and die of the wound.

The whole company trembled when they heard this terrible prediction. At this moment the young Fairy advanced from behind the tapestry and said, speaking that all might hear, "Comfort yourselves, King and Queen; your daughter shall not die of the wound. It is true that I have not sufficient power to undo entirely what my elder has done. The Princess will pierce her hand with a spindle, but instead of dying, she will only fall into a deep sleep, which will last a hundred years, at the end of which time a king's son will come and wake her."

The King immediately sent forth a proclamation forbidding everyone, on pain of death, either to spin with a spindle or to have spindles in their possession.

Fifteen or sixteen years had passed when, the King and Queen being closeted with their advisors, it happened that the Princess, while running about the castle one day and up the stairs from one room to the other, came to a little garret at the top of a turret, where an old woman sat alone, spinning with distaff and spindle, for this good woman had never heard the King's proclamation forbidding the use of the spindle.

"What are you doing there?" asked the Princess.

"I am spinning, my pretty child," answered the old woman, who did not know who she was.

"Oh, how pretty it is!" exclaimed the Princess. "How do you do it? Give it to me, that I may see if I can do it as well."

She had no sooner taken hold of the spindle than, being very hasty and rather thoughtless, and, moreover, the Fairies having ordained that it should be so, she pierced her hand with the point of it and fainted away. The poor old woman was in great distress and called for help. People came running from all quarters. They threw water in the

Princess's face; they unlaced her dress; they slapped her hands. But nothing would bring her to. The King, who had run upstairs at the noise, then remembered the prediction of the Fairies. He ordered the Princess to be carried into a beautiful room of the palace and laid on a bed embroidered with silver and gold.

The King gave orders that she was to be left to sleep there in quiet until the hour of her awakening should arrive. The good Fairy who had saved her life by condemning her to sleep for a hundred years approved of all he had done; but being gifted with great foresight, she bethought her that the Princess would feel very lost and bewildered on awaking and finding herself all alone in the old castle; so with her wand she touched everybody who was in the castle except the King and Queen: governesses, maids of honor, women of the bedchamber, gentlemen, officers, stewards, cooks, scullions, boys, guards, porters, pages, footmen. She also touched the horses that were in the stables with their grooms, the great mastiffs in the courtyard, and little Fluff, the pet dog of the Princess, who was on the bed beside her. As soon as she had touched them, they all fell asleep. Even the spits before the fire, hung with partridges and pheasants, and the very fire itself went to sleep. All this was done in a moment.

The King and Queen now kissed their dear daughter, who still slept on. Then, quitting the castle, they issued a proclamation forbidding any person whatsoever to approach it. These orders were unnecessary, for in a quarter of an hour there grew up around the park such a number of trees, large and small, of brambles and thorns interlacing each other, that neither man nor beast could have got through them, and nothing could be now seen of the castle but the tops of the turrets, and they only from a considerable distance. Nobody doubted that this also was some of the Fairy's handiwork, in order that the Princess might be protected from the curiosity of strangers during her long slumber.

When the hundred years had passed away, the King upon the throne was of a different family than that of the sleeping Princess; and his son, having been hunting in the neighborhood, inquired what towers they were that he saw above the trees of a very thick wood. Some said it was an old castle haunted by ghosts; others, that all the witches of the country held their midnight revels there. The more general opinion was that it was the abode of an Ogre who carried thither all the children he could catch in order to eat them at his leisure and without being pursued, he alone having the power of making his way through the wood.

The Prince did not know what to believe of all this until an old peasant said to him, "Prince, it is more than fifty years since I heard my father say that there was in that castle the most beautiful Princess ever seen; that she was to sleep for a hundred years, and would be awakened by a king's son."

The young Prince at these words felt himself all on fire. He had not a moment's doubt that he was the one chosen to accomplish this famous adventure, and urged to the deed by love and glory, he resolved without delay to see what would come of it.

Scarcely had he approached the wood when all those great trees, all those brambles and thorns, made way for him to pass of their own accord. He walked toward the castle, which he saw at the end of a long avenue, and he was somewhat surprised to find that none of his people had been able to follow him, the trees having closed up again as soon as he had passed. Nevertheless he continued to advance. He came to a large forecourt, where everything he saw might well have frozen his blood with terror. A frightful silence reigned around; death seemed everywhere present. On every side nothing was to be seen but the bodies of men and animals stretched out apparently lifeless.

He next passed through a large courtyard, ascended the staircase, and entered the guard room, where the guards stood drawn up in line and snoring their loudest. He traversed several rooms with ladies and gentlemen all asleep, some standing, others seated. At last he came to a room covered with gold, and there on a bed, the curtains of which were open on either side, he saw the most lovely sight he had ever looked upon—a Princess who appeared to be about fifteen or sixteen and whose dazzling beauty shone with a radiance that scarcely seemed to belong to this world. He approached, trembling and admiring, and knelt down beside her.

At that moment, the enchantment being ended, the Princess awoke, and gazing at him for the first time with unexpected tenderness, "Is it you, Prince?" she said. "I have waited long for you to come." The Prince, delighted at these words and still more by the tone in which they were uttered, knew not how to express his joy and gratitude. He assured her that he loved her better than himself.

In the meantime all the palace had been roused at the same time as the Princess. Everybody remembered his or her duty, and as they were not all in love, they were dying with hunger. The lady-in-waiting, as hungry as any of them, became impatient and announced loudly to the Princess that the meat was on the table. The Prince assisted the Princess to rise. She was fully dressed, and most magnificently, but he was careful not to tell her that she was dressed like his grandmother.

They passed into a hall of mirrors, where they supped, waited upon by the officers of the Princess. The violins and oboes played old but charming pieces of music, and after supper, without loss of time, the grand almoner married the royal lovers in the chapel of the castle.

Early next morning the Prince returned to the city, where he knew his father would be waiting anxiously for him. The Prince told him that he had lost his way in the forest while hunting and that he had slept in the hut of a woodcutter who had given him black bread and cheese to eat.

The King, his father, who was a simpleminded man, believed him, but his mother was not so easily satisfied. She noticed that he went hunting nearly every day and had always some story ready as an excuse when he had slept two or three nights away from home, and so she felt quite sure that he had a ladylove.

More than two years went by, and the Princess had two children: The first, who was a girl, was named Aurora; and the second, a son, was called Day, because he was still more beautiful than his sister.

The Queen, hoping to find out the truth from her son, often said to him that he ought to form some attachment, but he never dared to trust her with his secret. Although he loved her, he feared her, for she was of the race of Ogres, and the King had married her only on account of her great riches. It was even whispered about the court that she had the inclinations of an Ogress, and that when she saw little children passing, it was with the greatest difficulty that she restrained herself from pouncing upon them.

On the death of the King, which took place two years later, the Prince, being now his own master, made a public declaration of his marriage and went in great state to bring the Queen, his wife, to the palace. She made a magnificent entry into the capital with her two children, one on either side of her.

Some time afterward the new King went to war with his neighbor, the Emperor Cantalabute. He left the Queen, his mother, Regent of the Kingdom, earnestly recommending to her care his wife and children. He was likely to be all summer in the field, and he had no sooner left than the Queen Mother sent her daughter-in-law and the children to a country house in the wood so that she might more easily gratify her horrible longing. She followed them thither a few days after, and one evening she said to her head cook, "I will eat little Aurora for dinner tomorrow."

"Ah, madam!" exclaimed the cook.

"I will," said the Queen Mother, and she said it in the voice of an Ogress longing to eat fresh meat. "And I will have her served with my favorite sauce."

The poor man, seeing plainly that an Ogress was not to be trifled with, took his great knife and went up to little Aurora's room. She was then about four years old, and she came jumping and laughing to throw her arms about his neck and ask him for sweetmeats. He burst into tears, and the knife fell from his hands; then he went down again and into the farmyard, and there he killed a little lamb, which he served up with so delicious a sauce that his mistress assured him she had never eaten anything so excellent. In the meantime he had carried off little Aurora and given her to his wife, that she might hide her in the lodging that she occupied at the farther end of the farmyard. A week later the wicked Queen Mother said to her head cook, "I will eat little Day for supper." He made no reply, having decided in his own mind to deceive her as before.

He went in search of little Day and found him with a tiny foil in his hand, fencing with a great monkey, though he was only three years old. He carried the child to his wife, who hid him where she had hidden his sister, and then cooked a very tender baby goat in the place of little Day, which the Ogress thought wonderfully good. All had gone well enough so far, but one evening this wicked Queen Mother said to the head cook, "I should like to eat the Queen with the same sauce that I had with the children."

Then the poor cook was indeed in despair, for he did not know how he should be able to deceive her. The young Queen was over twenty years of age, without counting the hundred years she had slept, and no longer such tender food, although her skin was still white and beautiful. Where among all his animals should he find one old enough to take her place?

He resolved at last that, to save his own life, he would kill the Queen, and he went up to her room determined to carry out his purpose without delay. He worked himself up into a passion and entered the young Queen's room, dagger in hand. He did not wish, however, to take her by surprise, and so he repeated to her very respectfully the order he had received from the Queen Mother. "Do your duty," she said, stretching out her neck to him. "Obey the orders that have been given to you. I shall again see my children, my poor children, whom I loved so dearly." For she had thought them dead ever since they had been carried away from her without a word of explanation.

"No, no, madam!" replied the poor cook, touched to the quick. "You shall not die, and you shall see your children again, but it will be in my own house, where I have hidden them; I will again deceive the Queen Mother by serving up to her a young deer in your stead."

He led her forthwith to his own apartments. Then, leaving her to embrace her children and weep with them, he went and prepared a deer, which the Queen Mother ate at her supper with as much appetite as if it had been the young Queen. She exulted in her cruelty, intending to tell the King on his return that some ferocious wolves had devoured the Queen, his wife, and her two children.

One evening, while she was prowling as usual around the courts and poultry yards of the castle to inhale the smell of fresh meat, she overheard little Day crying in one of the lower rooms because the Queen, his mother, was about to spank him for being naughty, and she also heard little Aurora begging forgiveness for her brother. The Ogress recognized the voices of the Queen and her children, and furious at having been deceived, she gave orders, in a voice that made everybody tremble, that the next morning early there should be brought into the middle of the court a large cauldron, to be filled with toads, vipers, adders, and serpents, and that the Queen and her children, the head cook, his wife, and his maidservant should be thrown into it. She further commanded that they should be brought thither with their hands tied behind them.

There they stood, and the executioners were preparing to fling them into the cauldron, when the King, who was not expected back so soon, entered the courtyard on horseback. He had ridden posthaste, and in great astonishment asked what was the meaning of this horrible spectacle. No one dared tell him, and the Ogress, enraged at what she saw, flung herself head foremost into the cauldron, where she was instantly devoured by the horrid reptiles with which she had herself caused it to be filled. The King could not help being sorry for it; she was his mother; but he quickly consoled himself with his beautiful wife and children.

Little Red Riding Hood

There was once upon a time a little village girl, the prettiest ever seen or known, of whom her mother was dotingly fond. Her grandmother was even fonder of her still, and had a little red hood made for the child, which suited her so well that wherever she went she was known by the name of Little Red Riding Hood.

One day her mother, having baked some cakes, said to her, "Go and see how your grandmother is getting on, for I have been told she is ill; take her a cake and this little jar of butter." Whereupon Little Red Riding Hood started off without delay toward the village in which her grandmother lived. On her way she had to pass through a wood, and there she met that sly old fellow Mr. Wolf, who felt that he should very much like to eat her up on the spot, but was afraid to do so, as there were woodcutters at hand in the forest.

He asked her which way she was going, and the poor child, not knowing how dangerous it is to stop and listen to a wolf, answered, "I am going to see my grandmother, and am taking a cake and a little jar of butter, which my mother has sent her."

"Does she live far from here?" asked the Wolf.

"Oh, yes!" replied Little Red Riding Hood. "On the far side of the mill that you see down there; hers is the first house in the village."

"Well, I was thinking of going to visit her myself," rejoined the Wolf, "so I will take this path, and you take the other, and we will see which of us gets there first."

The Wolf then began running off as fast as he could along the shorter way, which he had

chosen, while the little girl went by the longer way and amused herself with stopping to gather nuts or run after butterflies, and with making little nosegays of all the flowers she could find.

It did not take the Wolf long to reach the grandmother's house. He knocked: *tap, tap*. "Who is there?"

"It is your granddaughter, Little Red Riding Hood," answered the Wolf, imitating the child's voice. "I have brought a cake and a little jar of butter, which my mother has sent you."

The good grandmother, who was ill in bed, called out, "Pull the cord, and the latch will go up." The Wolf pulled the cord, and the door opened. He leaped onto the poor old woman and ate her up in less than no time, for he had been three days without food. He then shut the door again and laid himself down in the grandmother's bed to wait for Little Red Riding Hood. Presently she came and knocked at the door: *tap, tap*.

"Who is there?"

Little Red Riding Hood was frightened at first, on hearing the Wolf's gruff voice, but thinking that her grandmother had a cold, she answered, "It is your granddaughter, Little Red Riding Hood. I have brought a cake and a little jar of butter, which my mother has sent you."

The Wolf called out, this time in rather a softer voice, "Pull the cord, and the latch will go up." Little Red Riding Hood pulled the cord, and the door opened.

When the Wolf saw her come in, he hid himself under the bedclothes and said to her, "Put the cake and the little jar of butter in the cupboard, and come into bed with me."

Little Red Riding Hood went to the bedside, and was very much astonished to see how different her grandmother looked from how she did when she was up and dressed.

"Grandmother," she exclaimed, "what long arms you have!"

"All the better to hug you with, my little girl."

"Grandmother, what long legs you have!"

"All the better to run with, child."

"Grandmother, what long ears you have!"

"All the better to hear with, child."

"Grandmother, what large eyes you have!"

"All the better to see with, child."

"Grandmother, what large teeth you have!"

"All the better to eat you with!" And saying these words, the wicked Wolf sprang out upon Little Red Riding Hood and ate her up.

Blue Beard

Once upon a time there was a man who had fine houses in town and country, gold and silver plate, embroidered furniture, and coaches gilt all over. But unfortunately this man had a blue beard, which made him look so ugly and terrible that there was not a woman or girl who did not run away from him.

One of his neighbors, a lady of rank, had two daughters who were perfectly beautiful. He proposed to marry one of them, leaving the mother to choose which of the two she would give him. Neither of the daughters, however, would marry a man with a blue beard. A further reason that they had for disliking him was that he had already been married several times, and nobody knew what had become of his wives. Blue Beard, in order to improve the acquaintance, took the girls, with their mother, three or four of their most intimate friends, and some other young people who resided in the neighborhood, to one of his country seats, where they spent an entire week. Nothing was thought of but excursions, hunting and fishing parties, balls, entertainments, and suppers. Nobody went to bed; the whole night was passed in games and playing merry tricks on one another. In short, all went off so well that the youngest daughter began to think that the beard of the master of the house was not so blue as it used to be and that he was a very worthy man. Indeed, she agreed to marry him, and immediately upon their return to town the marriage took place.

At the end of a month Blue Beard told his wife that he was obliged to take a journey that would keep him away from home for six weeks at least, as he had business of great importance to attend to. He begged her to amuse herself as well as she could during his absence, to invite her best friends and, if she liked, take them into the country, and wherever she was, to have the best of everything for the table.

"Here," said he to her, "are the keys of my two large storerooms. These are those of the chests in which the gold and silver plate not in general use is kept; these are the keys of the strongboxes in which I keep my money; these open the caskets that contain my jewels; and this is the master key of all the rooms. As for this little key, it is that of the closet at the end of the long gallery on the ground floor. Open everything and go everywhere except into that little closet, which I forbid you to enter, and I forbid you so strictly that if you should venture to open the door, there is nothing that you may not have to dread from my anger!" She promised to obey his orders to the letter, and after having embraced her, he got into his coach and set out on his journey.

The friends and neighbors of the young bride did not wait for her invitation, so eager were they to see all the rich treasures in the house, and not having ventured to visit her while her husband was at home, so frightened were they at his blue beard. They were soon to be seen running through all the rooms and into the closets and wardrobes, each of which was more beautiful than the last. Then they went upstairs to the storerooms, where they could not sufficiently express their admiration at the number and beauty of the hangings, the beds, the sofas, the cabinets, the elegant little stands, the tables, the mirrors in which they could see themselves from head to foot, framed, some with glass, some with silver, some with gilt metal, all of a costliness beyond what had ever before been seen. They never ceased envying the good fortune of their friend, who meanwhile took no pleasure in the sight of all these treasures, so great was her longing to go and open the door of the closet on the ground floor. Her curiosity at last reached such a pitch that, without stopping to consider how rude it was to leave her guests, she ran down a little back staircase leading to the closet in such haste that she nearly broke her neck two or three times before she reached the bottom. At the door of the closet she paused for a moment, calling to mind her husband's prohibition and reflecting that some trouble might fall upon her for her disobedience; but the temptation was so strong that she could not resist it. So she took the little key and with a trembling hand opened the door of the closet.

At first she could distinguish nothing, for the windows were closed. In a few minutes, however, she began to see that the floor was covered with blood, in which was reflected the bodies of several dead women hanging on the walls. These were all the wives of Blue Beard, who had killed them one after another. She was ready to die with fright, and the key, which she had taken out of the lock, fell from her hand.

After recovering her senses a little, she picked up the key, locked the door again, and went up to her room to try and compose herself; but she found it impossible to quiet her agitation.

She now perceived that the key of the closet was stained with blood; she wiped it two or three times, but the blood would not come off. In vain she washed it and even scrubbed it with sand and freestone, but the stain was still there, for the key was an enchanted one and there were no means of cleaning it completely; when the blood was washed off one side, it came back on the other.

Blue Beard returned that very evening and said that he had received letters on the road, telling him that the business on which he was going had been settled to his advantage.

His wife did all she could to make him believe she was delighted at his speedy return.

The next morning he asked her for his keys again. She gave them to him; but her hand trembled so, he had not much difficulty in guessing what had happened.

"How comes it," said he, "that the key of the closet is not with the others?"

"I must have left it," she replied, "upstairs on my table."

"Fail not," said Blue Beard, "to give it to me presently."

After several excuses she was obliged to go and fetch the key. Blue Beard, having examined it, said to his wife, "Why is there blood on this key?"

"I don't know," answered the poor wife, paler than death.

"You don't know!" rejoined Blue Beard. "I know well enough. You must needs go into the closet. Well, madam, you shall go in again and take your place among the ladies you saw there."

She flung herself at her husband's feet, weeping and begging his pardon with all the signs of true repentance at having disobeyed him. Her beauty and sorrow might have melted a rock, but Blue Beard had a heart harder than rock.

"You must die, madam," said he, "and at once."

"If I must die," she replied, looking at him with streaming eyes, "give me a little time to say my prayers."

"I give you half a quarter of an hour," answered Blue Beard. "Not a minute more."

As soon as she found herself alone, she called her sister and said to her, "Sister Anne"—for so she was named—"go up, I pray you, to the top of the tower and see if my brothers are not in sight. They promised they would come to visit me today, and if you see them, signal to them to make haste."

Sister Anne mounted to the top of the tower, and the poor, unhappy wife called to her from time to time, "Anne! Sister Anne! Do you not see anything coming?"

And Sister Anne answered her, "I see nothing but the dust turning gold in the sun and the grass growing green."

Meanwhile Blue Beard, with a large cutlass in his hand, called out with all his might to his wife, "Come down quickly, or I shall come up there!"

"One minute more, if you please," replied his wife, and then said quickly in a low voice, "Anne! Sister Anne! Do you not see anything coming?"

And Sister Anne answered, "I see nothing but the dust turning gold in the sun and the grass growing green."

"Come down quickly," roared Blue Beard, "or I shall come up there!"

"I am coming," answered his wife, and then called, "Anne! Sister Anne! Do you not see anything coming?"

"I see a great cloud of dust moving this way," said Sister Anne.

"Is it my brothers?"

"Alas, no, Sister! Only a flock of sheep."

"Will you not come down?" shouted Blue Beard.

"One minute more," replied his wife. And then she cried, "Anne! Sister Anne! Do you not see anything coming?"

"I see two horsemen coming this way," she replied, "but they are still a great distance off. Heaven be praised!" she exclaimed a moment afterward. "They are my brothers! I am making all the signs I can to hasten them."

Blue Beard began to roar so loudly that the whole house shook again. The poor wife went down and threw herself at his feet with weeping eyes and dishevelled hair. "It is of no use," said Blue Beard. "You must die!" Then, taking her by the hair with one hand, and raising the cutlass with the other, he was about to cut off her head.

The poor wife, turning toward him her dying eyes, begged him to give her one short moment to collect herself. "No, no," said he. "Commend yourself to heaven." And lifting his arm . . .

At this moment there was such a loud knocking at the gate that Blue Beard stopped short. It was opened, and two horsemen were immediately seen to enter who, drawing their swords, ran straight at Blue Beard. He recognized them as the brothers of his wife, one a dragoon, the other a musketeer, and he therefore fled at once, hoping to escape. But they pursued him so closely that they overtook him before he could reach the steps to his door, and, running their swords through his body, left him dead on the spot. The poor wife was almost as dead as her husband and had not strength to rise and embrace her brothers.

It was found that Blue Beard had left no heirs, and so his widow came into possession of all his property. She employed part of it in marrying her Sister Anne to a man who had long loved her; another part in buying captains' commissions for her two brothers; and with the remainder she married herself to a very worthy man, who made her forget the dreadful time she had passed with Blue Beard.

Master Cat

or *Puss in Boots*

A Miller bequeathed to his three sons all he possessed of worldly goods, which consisted only of his mill, his ass, and his Cat. It did not take long to divide the property, and neither notary nor attorney was called in; they would soon have eaten up the poor little patrimony. The eldest son had the mill; the second son, the ass; and the youngest had nothing but the Cat.

The latter was very disconsolate at having such a poor share of the inheritance. "My brothers," said he, "may be able to earn an honest livelihood by entering into partnership; but as for me, when I have eaten my Cat and made a muff of his skin, I must die of hunger."

The Cat, who had heard this speech, although he had not appeared to do so, said to him with a sedate and serious air, "Do not be troubled, master; you have only to give me a bag and get a pair of boots made for me in which I can go among the bushes, and you will see that you are not left so badly off as you believe." Though his master did not place much reliance on the Cat's words, he had seen him play such cunning tricks in catching rats and mice that he was not altogether without hope of being helped by him out of his distress.

As soon as the Cat had what he asked for, he boldly pulled on his boots and, hanging his bag around his neck, took the strings of it in his forepaws and started off for a warren where there were a great number of rabbits. He put some bran and sow thistles in his bag, and then, stretching himself out as if he were dead, he waited till some young rabbit, little versed in the wiles of the world, should come and poke his way into the bag in order to eat what was inside it.

He had hardly laid himself down before he had the pleasure of seeing a young scatterbrain of a rabbit get into the bag, whereupon Master Cat pulled the strings, caught it, and killed it without mercy. Proud of his prey, he went to the palace and asked to speak to the King. He was ushered upstairs and into the state apartment, and after making a low bow to the King, he said, "Sire, here is a wild rabbit, which my Lord the Marquis of Carabas"—for such was the title he had taken a fancy to give to his master—"has ordered me to present, with his duty, to your Majesty."

"Tell your master," replied the King, "that I thank him and am pleased with his gift."

Another day the Cat went and hid himself in the wheat, keeping the mouth of his bag open as before, and as soon as he saw that a brace of partridges had run inside, he pulled the strings and so took them both. He went immediately and presented them to the King, as he had the rabbits. The King was equally grateful at receiving the brace of partridges and ordered drink to be given to him.

For the next two or three months the Cat continued in this manner, taking presents of game at intervals to the King, as if from his master. One day, when he knew the King was going to drive on the banks of the river with his daughter, the most beautiful Princess in the world, he said to his master, "If you will follow my advice, your fortune is made; you have only to go and bathe in a part of the river I will point out to you, and then leave the rest to me."

The Marquis of Carabas did as his Cat advised him, without knowing what good would come of it. While he was bathing, the King passed by, and the Cat began to call out with all his might, "Help! Help! My Lord the Marquis of Carabas is drowning!" Hearing the cry, the King looked out of the coach window, and recognizing the Cat who had so often brought him game, he ordered his guards to fly to the help of my Lord the Marquis of Carabas. While they were getting the poor Marquis out of the river, the Cat went up to the royal coach and told the King that, while his master had been bathing, some robbers had come and carried off his clothes, although he had shouted "Stop, thief!" as loud as he could. (The Cat had hidden the clothes himself under a large stone.) The King immediately ordered the officers of his wardrobe to go and fetch one of his handsomest suits for my Lord the Marquis of Carabas. The King embraced him a thousand times, and as the fine clothes

they dressed him in set off his good looks—for he was handsome and well made—the Marquis of Carabas quite took the fancy of the King's daughter, and after he had cast two or three respectful and rather tender glances toward her, she fell very much in love with him. The King insisted upon his getting into the coach and accompanying them in their drive. The Cat, delighted to see that his plans were beginning to succeed, ran on before, and coming across some peasants who were mowing a meadow, he said to them, "You, good people who are mowing here. If you do not tell the King that this meadow you are mowing belongs to my Lord the Marquis of Carabas, you shall all be cut into pieces as small as minced meat." The King did not fail to ask the peasants whose meadow it was they were mowing.

"It belongs to my Lord the Marquis of Carabas," said all of them together, for the Cat's threat had frightened them.

"You have a fine property there," said the King to the Marquis of Carabas.

"As you say, sire," responded the Marquis of Carabas, "for it is a meadow that yields an abundant crop every year."

Master Cat, who still kept in advance of the party, came up to some reapers and said to them, "You, good people who are reaping in these fields. If you do not say that all this corn belongs to my Lord the Marquis of Carabas, you shall all be cut into pieces as small as minced meat."

The King, who passed by a minute afterward, wished to know to whom belonged all the cornfields he saw. "To my Lord the Marquis of Carabas," repeated the reapers, and the King again congratulated the Marquis on his property.

The Cat, still continuing to run before the coach, uttered the same threat to everyone he met, and the King was astonished at the great wealth of my Lord the Marquis of Carabas. Master Cat at length arrived at a fine castle, the owner of which was an Ogre, the richest Ogre ever known, for all the lands through which the King had driven belonged to the lord of this castle. The Cat took care to find out who the Ogre was and what he was able to do. Then he asked to speak with him, saying that he did not like to pass so near his castle without doing himself the honor of paying his respects to him. The Ogre received him as civilly as an Ogre can and made him sit down.

"I have been told," said the Cat, "that you have the power of changing yourself into all kinds of animals; that you could, for instance, transform yourself into a lion or an elephant."

" 'Tis true," said the Ogre abruptly. "And to prove it to you, you shall see me become a lion!"

The Cat was so frightened when he saw a lion in front of him that he quickly scrambled up into the gutter, not without difficulty and danger on account of his boots, which were worse than useless for walking on the tiles. Shortly afterward, seeing that the Ogre had resumed his natural form, the Cat climbed down again and admitted that he had been terribly frightened.

"I have also been assured," said the Cat, "but I cannot believe it, that you have the power besides of taking the form of the smallest animal; for instance, that of a rat or a mouse. I confess to you I hold this to be utterly impossible."

"Impossible!" exclaimed the Ogre. "You shall see!" And he immediately changed himself into a mouse and began running about the floor. The cat no sooner caught sight of it than he pounced upon it and ate it.

In the meantime the King, seeing the fine castle of the Ogre as he was driving past, thought he should like to go inside. The Cat, who heard the noise of the coach rolling over the drawbridge, ran to meet it and said to the King, "Your Majesty is welcome to the Castle of my Lord the Marquis of Carabas!"

"So, my Lord Marquis!" exclaimed the King. "This castle belongs to you? Nothing could be finer than this courtyard and all these buildings that surround it. Let us see the inside of it, if you please."

The Marquis offered his hand to the young Princess, and following the King, who led the way upstairs, they entered a grand hall, where they found prepared a magnificent repast, which the Ogre had ordered in expectation of some friends who were to have visited him that very day but who did not dare venture to enter when they heard the King was there.

The King was greatly delighted with the excellent qualities of my Lord the Marquis of Carabas, as was also his daughter, who became more than ever in love with him; and the

King, seeing what great wealth he possessed, said to him, after having drunk five or six gobletsful, "It depends entirely on yourself, my Lord Marquis, whether or not you become my son-in-law." The Marquis, making several profound bows, accepted the honor the King had offered him and that same day was married to the Princess.

The Cat became a great lord and never again ran after mice, except for his amusement.

The Fairies

There was once a widow who had two daughters. The elder was so like her mother in temper and face that to have seen the one was to have seen the other. They were both so disagreeable and proud that it was impossible to live with them. The younger, who was the exact portrait of her father in her kindly and polite ways, was as beautiful a girl as one could see. As we are naturally fond of those who resemble us, the mother doted on her elder daughter, while for the younger she had a most violent aversion and made her take her meals in the kitchen and work hard all day. Among other things that she was obliged to do, this poor child was forced to go twice a day to fetch water from a place a mile or more from the house and carry back a large jug filled to the brim. As she was standing one day by this spring, a poor woman came up to her and asked the girl to give her some water to drink.

"Certainly, my good woman," she replied, and the beautiful girl at once stooped and rinsed out the jug, and then, filling it with water from the clearest part of the spring, she held it up to the woman, continuing to support the jug, that she might drink with great comfort.

Having drunk, the woman said to her, "You are so beautiful, so good and kind, that I cannot refrain from conferring a gift upon you." For she was really a Fairy who had taken the form of a poor village woman in order to see how far the girl's kindheartedness would go. "This gift I make you," continued the Fairy: "that with every word you speak, a flower or a precious stone will fall from your mouth."

The girl had no sooner reached home than her mother began scolding her for being back so late. "I am sorry, Mother," said she, "to have been out so long," and as she spoke, there fell from her mouth six roses, two pearls, and two large diamonds.

The mother gazed at her in astonishment. "What do I see!" she exclaimed. "Pearls and diamonds seem to be dropping from her mouth! How is this, my daughter?"—it was the first time she had called her "daughter." The poor child related in all simplicity what had happened, letting fall quantities of diamonds in the course of her narrative. "I must certainly send my other daughter there," said the mother. "Look, Fanchon, see what falls from your sister's mouth when she speaks! Would you not be glad to receive a similar gift? All you have to do is to go and fetch water from the spring and, if an old woman asks you for some to drink, to give it her nicely and politely."

"I should like to see myself going to the spring," answered the rude, cross girl.

"I insist on your going," rejoined the mother, "and that at once."

The elder girl went off, still grumbling; with her she took the handsomest silver bottle she could find in the house.

She had no sooner arrived at the spring than she saw a lady, magnificently dressed, walking toward her from the wood, who approached and asked for some water to drink. It was the same Fairy who had appeared to the sister, but she had now put on the airs and apparel of a princess, as she wished to see how far this girl's rudeness would go.

"Do you think I came here just to draw water for you?" answered the arrogant and unmannerly girl. "I have, of course, brought this silver bottle on purpose for you to drink from, and all I have to say is—drink from it if you like!"

"You are scarcely polite," said the Fairy without losing her temper. "However, as you are so disobliging, I confer this gift upon you: that with every word you speak, a snake or a toad shall fall from your mouth."

Just then her mother caught sight of her, and she called out, "Well, my daughter!"

"Well, my mother!" replied the ill-tempered girl, throwing out as she spoke two vipers and a toad.

"Alack!" cried the mother. "What do I see? This is her sister's doing, but I will pay her back for it." And so saying, she ran toward the younger girl with intent to beat her. The unhappy girl fled from the house and went and hid herself in a neighboring forest.

The King's son, who was returning from hunting, met her and, seeing how beautiful she was, asked her what she was doing there all alone and why she was crying.

"Alas, sir! My mother has driven me from home."

The King's son, seeing five or six pearls and as many diamonds falling from her mouth as she spoke, asked her to explain how this was, and she told him all her tale. The King's son fell in love with her, and thinking that such a gift as she possessed was worth more than any ordinary dower brought by another, he carried her off to his father's palace and there married her.

As for her sister, she made herself so hated that her own mother drove her from the house. The miserable girl, having gone about in vain trying to find someone who would take her in, crept away into the corner of a wood and there died.

Cinderella

or *The Little Glass Slipper*

Once upon a time there was a nobleman who took for a second wife the haughtiest and proudest woman who had ever been seen. She had two daughters who resembled her in everything. The husband, on his side, had a daughter of unexampled gentleness and goodness.

The wedding was hardly over before the stepmother's ill humor broke out. She could not endure the young girl, whose good qualities made her own daughters appear still more detestable. She put her to do all the most menial work in the house. It was she who washed up the plates and dishes and cleaned the stairs, who scrubbed the stepmother's room and those of her daughters. She slept in a garret at the top of the house on a wretched straw mattress, while her sisters occupied rooms with inlaid floors and had the latest-fashion beds, and mirrors in which they could see themselves from head to foot. The poor girl bore everything with patience and did not dare complain to her father, who would only have scolded her, as he was entirely governed by his wife. When she had done her work, she was in the habit of going into the chimney corner and sitting down among the cinders, which caused her to be nicknamed Cindertail by the household in general. The second daughter, however, who was not quite so rude as her sister, called her Cinderella. Nevertheless Cinderella in her shabby clothes still looked a thousand times more beautiful than her sisters, magnificently dressed as they were.

It happened that the King's son gave a ball to which he invited everyone of position. Our two fine ladies were among those who received an invitation, for they had made a great

show in the neighborhood. They were now in great delight and very busy choosing the most becoming gowns and headdresses—a new mortification for poor Cinderella, for it was she who had to iron her sisters' fine linen and crimp their ruffles. No one talked of anything but the style in which they were to be dressed.

"I," said the elder, "will wear my red-velvet dress and my English point-lace trimmings."

"I," said the younger, "shall wear only my usual petticoat, but to make up for that, I shall put on my gold-flowered cloak and my clasp of diamonds, which are none of the least valuable." They sent for a first-rate milliner, that their caps might be made to fashion, and they bought their patches from the best maker. They called Cinderella to give them her opinion, for her taste was excellent. Cinderella gave them the best advice in the world and even offered to dress their hair for them, which they were very willing she should do.

While she was busy with the hairdressing, they said to her, "Cinderella, should you be very glad to go to the ball?"

"Alas! You only make fun of me; such a thing would not be suitable for me at all."

"You are right; they would indeed laugh to see a Cindertail at the ball!"

Any other than Cinderella would have dressed their hair awry, but she had a good disposition and arranged it for both of them to perfection. They could eat nothing for nearly two days, so transported were they with joy. More than a dozen laces were broken in making their waists as small as possible, and they were continually before their looking glasses. At last the happy day arrived. They set off, and Cinderella followed them with her eyes as long as she could. When they were out of sight, she began to cry.

Her Godmother, who saw her all in tears, asked her what was the matter. "I should so like— I should so like—" She sobbed so violently that she could not finish the sentence.

"You would so like to go to the ball, is not that it?"

"Alas! Yes," said Cinderella, sighing.

"Well, if you will be a good girl, I will undertake that you shall go." She took her into her room and said to her, "Go into the garden and bring me a pumpkin." Cinderella went at once, gathered the finest she could find, and brought it to her Godmother, wondering the while how a pumpkin could enable her to go to the ball. Her Godmother scooped it out and, having left nothing but the rind, struck it with her wand, and the pumpkin was immediately changed into a beautiful coach, gilt all over. She then went and looked into the mousetrap, where she found six mice, all alive. She told Cinderella to lift the door of the mousetrap a little, and to each mouse as it ran out she gave a tap with her wand, and the mouse was immediately changed into a fine horse, so that at last there stood ready a handsome train of six horses of a beautiful dappled mouse-gray color. Cinderella then brought her the rattrap, in which there were three large rats. The Fairy chose one from the three on account of its ample beard, and having touched it, it was changed into a fat coachman with the finest whiskers that ever were seen. She then said, "Go into the garden, and there, behind the watering pot, you will find six lizards. Bring them to me." Cinderella had no sooner brought them than the Godmother changed them into six footmen, with their liveries all covered with lace, who immediately jumped up behind the coach and hung on to it as if they had done nothing else all their lives. The Fairy then said to Cinderella, "Well, there is something in which to go to the ball. Are you not well pleased?"

"Yes, but am I to go in these dirty old clothes?" Her Godmother touched her lightly with her wand, and in the same instant her dress was changed into one of gold and silver covered with precious stones. She then gave her a pair of glass slippers, the prettiest in the world. When Cinderella was thus attired, she got into the coach. But her Godmother told her, above all things, not to stay past midnight, warning her that if she remained at the ball a minute longer, her coach would again become a pumpkin; her horses, mice; her footmen, lizards; and her clothes turn again into her old ones. She promised her Godmother that she would not fail to leave the ball before midnight, and drove off almost delirious with joy.

The King's son, who was informed that a grand Princess had arrived whom nobody knew, ran to receive her. He escorted her out of the coach and led her into the hall where the guests were assembled. There was immediately a dead silence; the dancing stopped and the fiddlers ceased to play, so engaged did everyone become in gazing upon the wonderful beauty of the unknown lady. Nothing was heard but a general murmur of "Oh! How lovely she is!" The King himself, old as he was, could not take his eyes from her and observed to the Queen that it was a long time since he had seen so lovely and amiable a person. All the ladies were intently occupied in examining her headdress and her clothes, that they might order some like them the very next day, provided that they might be able to find materials as costly and workpeople sufficiently clever to make them up.

The King's son conducted her to the most honorable seat, and then led her out to dance. She danced so gracefully that everybody's admiration of her was increased. A very grand supper was served, of which the Prince ate not a morsel, so absorbed was he in the contemplation of her beauty. She seated herself beside her sisters and showed them a thousand civilities. She shared with them the oranges and citrons that the Prince had given her, at which they were greatly surprised, for she appeared a perfect stranger to them. While they were thus talking together, Cinderella heard the clock strike three quarters past eleven. She at once made a deep curtsy to the company and left as quickly as she could. As soon as she reached home, she went to find her Godmother and, after having thanked her, said she much wished to go to the ball again the next day, because the King's son had invited her. She was telling her Godmother all that had passed at the ball when the two sisters knocked at the door. Cinderella went and opened it. "How late you are!" said she to them, yawning, rubbing her eyes, and then stretching herself as if she had but just awoken, although she had had no inclination to sleep since parting from them.

"If you had been at the ball," said one of her sisters to her, "you would not have been weary of it. There came to it the most beautiful Princess—the most beautiful that ever was seen. She paid us many attentions and gave us oranges and citrons." Cinderella was beside herself with delight. She asked them the name of the Princess, but they replied that nobody knew her, that the King's son was much puzzled about it, and that he would give everything in the world to know who she was.

Cinderella smiled and said, "She was very lovely, then? How fortunate you are! Could not I get a sight of her? Alas! Miss Javotte, lend me the yellow gown you wear every day."

"Truly," said Miss Javotte, "I like that! Lend one's gown to a dirty Cindertail like you! I should be mad indeed!" Cinderella fully expected this refusal and was rejoiced at it, for she would not have known what to do if her sister had lent her the gown.

The next day the sisters went again to the ball, and Cinderella also, but still more splendidly dressed than before. The King's son never left her side or ceased saying tender things to her. Cinderella found the evening passing very pleasantly and forgot her Godmother's warning, so that she heard the clock begin to strike twelve while still thinking that it was not yet eleven. She rose and fled as lightly as a fawn. The Prince followed her but could not overtake her. She dropped one of her glass slippers, which the Prince carefully picked up. Cinderella reached home almost breathless, without coach or footmen, and in her shabby clothes, with nothing remaining of her finery but one of her little slippers, the fellow of that which she had dropped.

The guards at the palace gate were asked if they had not seen a Princess pass through. They answered that they had seen no one pass but a poorly dressed girl who had more the appearance of a peasant than of a lady.

When the two sisters returned from the ball, Cinderella asked them if they had been as much entertained as before and if the beautiful lady had been present. They said yes, but that she had fled as soon as it had struck twelve.

A few days afterward the King's son caused it to be proclaimed by sound of trumpet that he would marry her whose foot would exactly fit the slipper. They began by trying it on the princesses, then on the duchesses, and so on throughout the court; but in vain. It was taken to the two sisters, who did their utmost to force one of their feet into the slipper, but they could not manage to do so. Cinderella, who was looking on, and who recognized the slipper, said laughingly, "Let me see if it will not fit me." Her sisters began to laugh and ridicule her. The gentleman of the court who had been entrusted to try the slipper, having looked attentively at Cinderella and seeing that she was very beautiful, said that it was only fair that her request should be granted, as he had received orders to try the slipper on all maidens without exception. He made Cinderella sit down, and putting the slipper to her little foot, he saw it slip on easily and fit like wax. Great was the astonishment of the two sisters, but it was still greater when Cinderella took the other little slipper out of her pocket and put it on her other foot. At that moment the Godmother appeared and gave a tap with her wand to Cinderella's clothes, which became still more magnificent than those she had worn before.

The two sisters then recognized in her the beautiful person they had seen at the ball.

They threw themselves at her feet to beg for forgiveness for all the ill treatment she had suffered from them. Cinderella raised and embraced them, said that she forgave them with all her heart, and begged them to love her dearly in the future. She was conducted, dressed as she was, to the young Prince. He found her more charming than ever, and a few days afterward he married her. Cinderella, who was as kind as she was beautiful, gave her sisters apartments in the palace and married them the very same day to two great lords of the court.

Riquet with the Tuft

Once upon a time there was a Queen who had a son so ugly and misshapen that it was doubted for a long time whether his form was really human. A Fairy who was present at his birth affirmed, nevertheless, that he would be worthy to be loved, as he would have an excellent wit, and by virtue of the gift she had bestowed upon him, he would be able to impart equal intelligence to the one whom he loved best. All this was some consolation to the poor Queen, who was much distressed at having brought so ugly a little monkey into the world. It is true that the child was no sooner able to speak than he said a thousand pretty things and that in all his ways there was a certain air of intelligence with which everyone was charmed.

I had forgotten to say that he was born with a little tuft of hair on his head, and so he came to be called Riquet with the Tuft; for Riquet was the family name.

About seven or eight years later, the Queen of a neighboring kingdom had two daughters. The elder was fairer than the day, and the Queen was so delighted that it was feared some harm might come to her from her great joy. The same Fairy who had assisted at the birth of little Riquet was present upon this occasion, and in order to moderate the joy of the Queen, she told her that this little Princess would have no gifts of mind at all and that she would be as stupid as she was beautiful. The Queen was greatly mortified on hearing this, but shortly after she was even more annoyed when her second little daughter was born and proved to be extremely ugly.

"Do not distress yourself, madam," said the Fairy to her. "Your daughter will find compensation, for she will have so much intelligence, her lack of beauty will scarcely be perceived."

"Heaven send it may be so," replied the Queen. "But are there no means whereby a little more understanding might be given to the elder, who is so lovely?"

"I can do nothing for her in the way of intelligence, madam," said the Fairy, "but everything in the way of beauty. As, however, there is nothing in my power I would not do to give you comfort, I will bestow on her the power of conferring beauty on any man or woman who shall please her."

As these two Princesses grew up, their endowments also became more perfect, and nothing was talked of anywhere but the beauty of the elder and the intelligence of the younger. It is true that their defects also greatly increased with their years. The younger became uglier every moment and the elder more stupid every day. She either made no answer when she was spoken to or else said something foolish. With this she was so clumsy that she could not even place four pieces of china on a mantelshelf without breaking one of them, or drink a glass of water without spilling half of it on her dress.

Notwithstanding the attraction of beauty, the younger, in whatever society they might be, nearly always bore away the palm from her sister. At first everyone went up to the more beautiful to gaze at and admire her, but they soon left her for the cleverer one, to listen to her many pleasant and amusing sayings. And people were astonished to find that in less than a quarter of an hour the elder had not a soul near her, while all the company had gathered around the younger.

The elder, though very stupid, noticed this and would have given without regret all her beauty for half the sense of her sister. Discreet as she was, the Queen could not help often reproaching her elder daughter with her stupidity, which made the poor Princess ready to die of grief.

One day, when she had gone by herself into a wood to weep over her misfortune, she saw approaching her a little man of very ugly and unpleasant appearance, but magnificently dressed. It was the young Prince Riquet with the Tuft, who, having fallen in love with her from seeing her portraits, which were sent all over the world, had left his father's kingdom that he might have the pleasure of beholding her and speaking to her. Enchanted at meeting her thus alone, he addressed her with all the respect and politeness imaginable.

Having remarked, after paying her the usual compliments, that she was very melancholy, he said to her, "I cannot understand, madam, how a person so beautiful as you are can be so unhappy as you appear; for although I can boast of having seen an infinite number of beautiful people, I can say with truth that I have never seen one whose beauty could be compared with yours."

"You are pleased to say so, sir," replied the Princess, and there she stopped.

"Beauty," continued Riquet, "is so great an advantage that it ought to take the place of every other, and possessed of it, I see nothing that can have power to afflict one."

"I would rather," said the Princess, "be as ugly as you are and have intelligence, than possess the beauty I do and be so stupid as I am."

"There is no greater proof of intelligence, madam, than the belief that we have it not; it is the nature of that gift that the more we have, the more we believe ourselves to be without it."

"I do not know how that may be," said the Princess, "but I know well enough that I am very stupid, and that is the cause of the grief that is killing me."

"If that is all that troubles you, madam, I can easily put an end to your sorrow."

"And how would you do that?" said the Princess.

"I have the power, madam," said Riquet with the Tuft, "to give as much intelligence as it is possible to possess to the person whom I love best; and as you, madam, are that person, it will depend entirely upon yourself whether or not you become gifted with this amount of intelligence, provided that you are willing to marry me."

The Princess was struck dumb with astonishment and replied not a word.

"I see," said Riquet with the Tuft, "that this proposal troubles you, and I am not surprised, but I will give you a full year to consider it."

The Princess had so little sense, and at the same time was so anxious to have a great deal, that she thought the end of that year would never come; so she at once accepted the offer that was made her.

She had no sooner promised Riquet with the Tuft that she would marry him that day twelve months than she felt herself quite another person. She found she was able to say whatever she pleased with a readiness past belief, and to say it in a clever but easy, charming, and natural manner. She immediately began a sprightly and well-sustained conversation with Riquet with the Tuft and was so brilliant in her talk that Riquet with the Tuft began to think he had given her more wit than he had reserved for himself.

On the Princess's return to the palace, the whole court was puzzled to account for a change so sudden and extraordinary. All the court was in a state of joy not to be described. The younger sister alone was not altogether pleased, for having lost her superiority over her sister in the way of intelligence, she now appeared by her side as only a very unpleasing-looking person.

The King began to be guided by his elder daughter's advice and at times even held his council in her apartments. The news of the change of affairs was spread abroad, and all the young princes of the neighboring kingdoms exerted themselves to gain her affection, and nearly all of them asked her hand in marriage. She found none of them, however, intelligent enough to please her, and she listened to all of them without engaging herself to one.

At length arrived a Prince so rich and powerful, so clever and so handsome, that she could not help listening willingly to his addresses. Her father, having perceived this, told her that he left her at perfect liberty to choose a husband for herself and that she had only to make known her decision. As the more intelligence we possess, the more difficulty we find in making up our mind on such a matter as this, she begged her father, after having thanked him, to allow her time to think about it.

She went, by chance, to walk in the same wood in which she had met Riquet with the Tuft, in order to meditate more uninterruptedly over what she had to do. While she was walking deep in thought, she heard a dull sound beneath her feet, as of many persons running to and fro and busily occupied.

Having listened more attentively, she heard one say, "Bring me that saucepan"; another, "Give me that kettle"; another, "Put some wood on the fire." At the same moment the ground opened, and she saw beneath her what appeared to be a large kitchen full of cooks, scullions, and all sorts of servants necessary for the preparation of a magnificent banquet. There came forth a band of about twenty to thirty cooks, who went and established themselves in an avenue of the wood at a very long table and who, each with the larding pin

in his hand and the tail of his fur cap over his ear, set to work, keeping time to a harmonious song.

The Princess, astonished at this sight, stopped the men and asked them for whom they were working.

"Madam," replied the chief among them, "for Prince Riquet with the Tuft, whose marriage will take place tomorrow." The Princess, still more surprised than she was before and suddenly recollecting that it was just a twelvemonth from the day on which she had promised to marry Prince Riquet with the Tuft, was overcome with trouble and amazement. The reason of her not having remembered her promise was that when she made it, she had been a very foolish person, and when she became gifted with the new mind that the Prince had given her, she had forgotten all her follies.

She had not taken another thirty steps when Riquet with the Tuft presented himself before her, gaily and splendidly attired like a prince about to be married. "You see, madam," said he, "I keep my word punctually, and I doubt not that you have come hither to keep yours and to make me, by the giving of your hand, the happiest of men."

"I confess to you frankly," answered the Princess, "that I have not yet made up my mind on that matter and that I do not think I shall ever be able to do so in the way you wish."

"You astonish me, madam," said Riquet with the Tuft.

"I have no doubt I do," said the Princess. "And assuredly, had I to deal with a stupid person, with a man without intelligence, I should feel greatly perplexed. 'A Princess is bound by her word,' he would say to me, 'and you must marry me since you have promised to do so.' But as the person to whom I speak is, of all men in the world, the one of greatest sense and understanding, I am certain he will listen to reason. You know that, when I was no better than a fool, I nevertheless could not decide to marry you. How can you expect, now that I have the mind you have given me, which renders me much more difficult to please than before, that I should take today a resolution that I could not take then? If you seriously thought of marrying me, you did very wrong to take away my stupidity and so enable me to see more clearly than I saw then."

"If a man without intelligence," replied Riquet with the Tuft, "who reproached you with your breach of promise might have a right, as you have just intimated, to be treated with indulgence, why would you wish, madam, that I should receive less consideration in a matter that affects the entire happiness of my life? Is it reasonable that persons of intellect should be in a worse position than those who have none? Can you assert this—you who have so much and who so earnestly desired to possess it? But let us come to the point, if you please. Setting aside my ugliness, is there anything in me that displeases you? Are you dissatisfied with my birth, my understanding, my temper, or my manners?"

"Not in the least," replied the Princess. "I admire in you everything you have mentioned."

"If that is so," rejoined Riquet with the Tuft, "I shall soon be happy, as you have it in your power to make me the most pleasing looking of men."

"How can that be done?" asked the Princess.

"It can be done," said Riquet with the Tuft, "if you love me sufficiently to wish that it should be. And in order, madam, that you should have no doubt about it, know that the same Fairy who on the day I was born endowed me with the power to give intelligence to the person I chose gave you also the power to render handsome the man you should love and on whom you should wish to bestow this favor."

"If such be the fact," said the Princess, "I wish with all my heart that you should become the handsomest and most lovable Prince in the world, and I bestow the gift on you to the fullest extent in my power."

The Princess had no sooner pronounced these words than Riquet with the Tuft appeared to her eyes, of all men in the world, the handsomest, the best made, and most attractive she had ever seen.

There are some who assert that it was not the spell of the Fairy but love alone that caused this change. They say that the Princess, having reflected on the perseverance of her lover, on his prudence, and on all the good qualities of his heart and mind, no longer saw the deformity of his body or the ugliness of his features; that his hump appeared to her nothing more than a good-natured shrug of his shoulders; and that instead of noticing, as she had done, how badly he limped, she saw in him only a certain lounging air that charmed her. They say also that his eyes, which squinted, only seemed to her the more brilliant for this; and that the crookedness of his glance was to her merely expressive of his great love; and finally that his great red nose had in it, to her mind, something martial and heroic. However this may be, the Princess promised on the spot to marry him provided he obtained the consent of the King, her father. The King, having learned that his daughter entertained a great regard for Riquet with the Tuft, whom he knew also to be a very clever and wise Prince, received him with pleasure as his son-in-law. The wedding took place the next morning, as Riquet with the Tuft had foreseen, and according to the orders that he had given a long time before.

Tom Thumb

Once upon a time there was a woodcutter and his wife who had seven boys. The eldest was but ten years old, and the youngest only seven. People wondered that the woodcutter had so many children so near in age, but the fact was that several of them were twins. He and his wife were very poor, and their seven children were a great burden to them, as not one of them was yet able to earn his livelihood. What troubled them still more was that the youngest was very delicate and seldom spoke, which they considered a proof of stupidity rather than of good sense. He was very diminutive and, when first born, scarcely bigger than one's thumb, and so they called him Tom Thumb.

This poor child was the scapegoat of the house and was blamed for everything that happened. Nevertheless he was the shrewdest and most sensible of all his brothers, and if he spoke little, he listened a great deal.

There came a year of bad harvest and a famine. One evening, when they were all in bed and the woodcutter was sitting over the fire with his wife, he said to her, with an aching heart, "You see plainly that we can no longer find food for our children. I cannot let them die of hunger before my very eyes, and I have made up my mind to take them to the wood tomorrow and there lose them, which will be easily done, for while they are busy tying up the branches, we have only to run away unseen by them."

"Ah!" exclaimed the woodcutter's wife. "Can you find the heart to lose your own children?" In vain her husband represented to her their great poverty; she would not consent to the deed. She was poor, but she was their mother. After a while, however, having thought over the misery it would be to her to see them die of hunger, she assented to her husband's proposal and went weeping to bed.

Tom Thumb had overheard all they said, for having found out as he lay in his bed that they were talking of their affairs, he got up quietly and crept under his father's stool so as to listen to what they were saying without being seen. He went to bed again but did not sleep a wink the rest of the night, thinking what he should do. He got up early and went down to the banks of the stream; there he filled his pockets with small white pebbles, and then returned home. They set out all together, and Tom Thumb said not a word to his brothers of what he had overheard. They entered a very thick forest wherein at ten paces distant they could not see one another. The woodcutter began to cut wood and the children to pick up brushwood. The father and mother, seeing them busy at work, gradually stole farther and farther away from them, and then suddenly ran off down a little winding path.

When the children found themselves all alone, they began to scream and cry with all their might. Tom Thumb let them scream, well knowing how he could get home again, for on their way to the forest he had dropped all along the road the little white pebbles he had in his pockets. He then said to them, "Have no fear, brothers. My father and mother have left us here, but I will take you safely home; only follow me." And he led them back to the house by the same road that they had taken to the forest. They were afraid to go inside at once, but placed themselves close to the door to listen.

It chanced that just at the moment when the woodcutter and his wife reached home, the lord of the manor sent them ten crowns, which he had owed them a long time and which they had given up all hope of receiving. This was new life to them, for the poor things were actually starving. The woodcutter immediately sent his wife to the butcher's, and as it was many a day since they had tasted meat, she bought three times as much as was sufficient for two people's supper. When they had appeased their hunger, the woodcutter's wife said, "Alas! Where now are our poor children? They would fare merrily on what we have left. But it was you, William, who would lose them. Truly did I say we should repent it. What are they now doing in the forest? Alas! Heaven help me! The wolves have perhaps already devoured them. Cruel man that you are!"

The woodcutter began at last to lose his temper, for she repeated over twenty times that they would repent the deed and that she had said it would be so. He threatened to beat her if she did not hold her tongue. The wife was all in tears. "Alas! Where are now my children, my poor children?"

She uttered her cry at last so loudly that the children, who were at the door, heard her and began to call out all together, "Here we are! Here we are!"

She rushed to the door to open it and, embracing them, exclaimed, "How thankful I am to see you again, my dear children! You are very tired and hungry; and you, little Peter, how dirty you are! Come here and let me wash you." Peter was her eldest son, and she loved him better than all the rest. They sat down to supper and ate with an appetite that delighted their father and mother, to whom they related how frightened they had been in the forest, and they all kept on speaking at the same time.

The good people were overjoyed to see their children once more, and their joy lasted as long as the ten crowns. When the money was spent, however, they fell back into their former state of misery and resolved to lose their children again; and to make quite sure of doing so this time, they determined to lead them much farther from home.

They could not talk of this so secretly but that they were overheard by Tom Thumb, who reckoned upon being able to get out of the difficulty by the same means as he had the first time; but though he got up very early to collect the little pebbles, he did not succeed in his object, for he found the house door double-locked. He was at his wit's end what to do, when his mother handed each of them a piece of bread for their breakfast; it occurred to him that he might make the bread take the place of the pebbles by strewing crumbs along the path as they went, and so he put his piece in his pocket. The father and mother led them into the thickest and darkest part of the forest, and as soon as they had done so, they turned into a bypath and left them there. Tom Thumb did not trouble himself much, for he believed he could easily find his way back by help of the crumbs that he had scattered wherever he had passed; but he was greatly surprised to find not a single crumb left—the birds had come and picked them all up. The poor children were now, indeed, in great distress; the farther they wandered, the deeper they plunged into the forest. Night came on, and a great wind arose that filled them with terror. They fancied they heard nothing on every side but the howling of wolves running toward them to devour them. They scarcely dared to speak or look behind them. Then there came a heavy rain, which drenched them to the skin. They slipped at every step, tumbling into the mud. Tom Thumb climbed up a tree to try if he could see anything from the top of it. Having looked about on all sides, he saw a little light, like that of a candle, but it was a long way off, on the other side of the forest. He came down again, and when he had reached the ground, he could no longer see the light. He was in despair at this, but having walked on with his brothers for some time in the direction of the light, he caught sight of it again as they emerged from the forest.

At length they reached the house where the candle was shining, not without many alarms, for often they lost sight of it altogether and always when they went down into the hollows. They knocked loudly at the door, and a good woman came to open it. She asked them what they wanted. Tom Thumb told her they were poor children who had lost their way in the forest and who begged a night's lodgings for charity's sake.

The woman, seeing they were all so pretty, began to weep and said to them, "Alas! My poor children, to what a place have you come! Know you not that this is the house of an Ogre who eats little children?"

"Alas!" replied Tom Thumb, who trembled from head to foot, as indeed did all his brothers. "What shall we do? We shall certainly all be eaten up by the wolves tonight if you do not give us shelter. Perhaps the Ogre may have pity upon us if you are kind enough to ask him."

The Ogre's wife, who thought that she might be able to hide them from her husband till the next morning, let the children come in and led them where they could warm themselves by a good fire, for there was a whole sheep on the spit roasting for the Ogre's supper.

Just as they were beginning to get warm, they heard two or three loud knocks at the door. It was the Ogre, who had come home. His wife immediately made the children hide under the bed and went to open the door. The Ogre first asked if his supper was ready and if she had drawn the wine, and with that he sat down to his meal. The mutton was all but raw, but he liked it all the better for that. He sniffed right and left, saying that he smelt fresh meat.

"It must be the calf I have just skinned," said his wife.

"I tell you, I smell fresh meat," replied the Ogre, giving an angry glance at his wife. "There is something here I do not understand." With these words he rose from the table and went straight toward the bed. "Ah!" he exclaimed. "So this is the way in which you would deceive me, you wretched woman! I do not know what hinders me from eating you also! It is well for you that you are such an old creature! But here is some game that comes in handy and will serve to feast three of my Ogre friends, who are soon coming to pay me a visit."

He dragged the children from under the bed one after the other. They fell upon their knees, begging for mercy, but they had to deal with the most cruel of all the Ogres, who, far from feeling pity for them, devoured them already with his eyes and said to his wife that they would be dainty bits when she had made a good sauce for them. He went and took up a large knife, and as he came toward the children again, he whetted it on a long stone that he held in his left hand.

He had already seized one of them when his wife said to him, "Why are you doing that at this hour of night? Will it not be time enough tomorrow?"

"Hold your peace," replied the Ogre. "They will be the more tender."

"But you have already too much food," continued his wife. "Here are a calf, two sheep, and half a pig."

"You are right," said the Ogre. "Give them a good supper, that they may keep plump, and then put them to bed."

The good woman was rejoiced and brought them plenty of supper; but they could not eat, they were so overcome with fright. As for the Ogre, he seated himself to drink again, delighted to think he had such a treat in store for his friends. He drained a dozen goblets more than usual, which made him feel sleepy and heavy and obliged him to go to bed.

The Ogre had seven daughters who were still young children. These little Ogresses had the most beautiful complexions, as they lived on fresh meat like their father; but they had very small, round gray eyes, hooked noses, and very large mouths, with long teeth exceedingly sharp and wide apart. They were not very wicked as yet; but they promised to become so, for they had already begun to bite little children that they might suck their

blood. They had been sent to bed early and were all seven in a large bed, each wearing a crown of gold on her head. In the same room was another bed of the same size. It was in this bed that the Ogre's wife put the seven little boys to sleep, after which she went to bed herself.

Tom Thumb, who had noticed that the Ogre's daughters had golden crowns on their heads and who was afraid that the Ogre might repent of not having killed him and his brothers that evening, got up in the middle of the night. Taking off his own nightcap and those of his brothers, he went very softly and placed them on the heads of the Ogre's daughters, first taking off their golden crowns, which he put on his brothers and himself, in order that the Ogre might mistake them for his daughters, and his daughters for the boys whom he wanted to kill.

Everything turned out as Tom Thumb had expected. The Ogre awoke at midnight and regretted having put off till the morning what he might have done the evening before. He therefore jumped suddenly out of bed, and seizing his great knife, "Let us go and see," said he, "how the young rogues are getting on! I will not think twice about it this time." So he stole on tiptoes up to his daughters' bedroom and went up to the bed in which lay the little boys, who were all asleep except Tom Thumb, who was dreadfully frightened when the Ogre put his hand on his head to feel it, as he had in turn felt those of his brothers. The Ogre, feeling the golden crowns, said, "Truly, I was about to do a pretty piece of work! It's plain I drank too much wine last night." He then went to the bed where his daughters slept, and having felt the little nightcaps that belonged to the boys, "Aha!" cried he. "Here are our fine young fellows. Let us to work boldly!" So saying, he without pause cut the throats of his seven daughters.

Well satisfied with his deed, he returned and lay down beside his wife. As soon as Tom Thumb heard the Ogre snoring, he awoke his brothers and bade them dress themselves quickly and follow him. They crept down into the garden and jumped over the wall. They ran nearly all night long, trembling the whole time and not knowing whither they were going. The Ogre, awaking in the morning, said to his wife, "Go upstairs and dress those young scamps you took in last night." The Ogress was astonished at her husband's kindness, never guessing what he meant and only fancying that he wished her to go and put on their clothes. She went upstairs, where she was horrified to find that her own children had been killed. The first thing she did was to faint. The Ogre, fearing that his wife would be too long over the job he had given her to do, went upstairs to help her. His surprise was not less than had been his wife's, when his eyes fell on the frightful spectacle.

"Ah! What have I done?" he exclaimed. "The young wretches shall pay for it, and that at once." He threw a jugful of water in his wife's face and, having brought her to, said, "Quick! Fetch me my seven-league boots, that I may go after them and catch them."

He set out and, after running in every direction, came at last upon the track of the poor children, who were not more than a hundred yards from their father's house. They saw the Ogre striding from hill to hill and stepping over rivers as easily as if they were the smallest brooks. Tom Thumb, who had caught sight of a hollow rock close by where they were, hid his brothers in it and crept in after them, keeping his eye on the Ogre all the while. The Ogre, feeling very tired with his long journey to no purpose, thought he should like to rest and by chance sat down on the very rock in which the little boys had concealed themselves. As he was quite worn out, he did not rest long before he fell asleep, and began to snore so dreadfully that the poor children were not less frightened than they were when he took up the great knife to cut their throats.

Tom Thumb was not so much alarmed, and told his brothers to run quickly into the house while the Ogre was sound asleep, and not to be uneasy about him. They took his advice and soon reached home.

Tom Thumb then, going up to the Ogre, gently pulled off his boots and put them on himself. The boots were very large and very long; but as they were enchanted boots, they had the power of becoming larger or smaller according to the leg of the person who wore them, so that they fitted him as if they had been made for him. He went straight to the Ogre's house, where he found the wife weeping over her murdered daughters.

"Your husband," said Tom Thumb to her, "is in great danger, for he has been seized by a band of robbers who have sworn to kill him if he does not give them all his gold and silver. Just as they had their daggers at his throat, he saw me and begged me to come and tell you what had happened to him, and sent word that you were to give me all his ready money without keeping back any of it, as otherwise they will kill him without mercy. As time

pressed, he insisted on my taking his seven-league boots, which you see I have on, in order that I might make haste and also that you might be sure I was not deceiving you."

The good woman, very much alarmed, immediately gave him all the money she could find. Tom Thumb, thus laden with all the Ogre's wealth, hastened back to his father's house, where he was received with great joy.

A Note on the Illustrations

To create the illustrations in this book, Michael Hague used a variety of media. He started each painting by creating a small sketch. From the sketches, larger drawings were made, and more detail was added. At this stage, models were sometimes used to create natural, lifelike poses. Mr. Hague then transferred the pencil drawings onto #114 watercolor boards at approximately one and a half times the size at which they are reproduced in the book. The pencil outlines were next inked over with a Rapidograph pen, adding shading where necessary. Using Winsor & Newton watercolors and brushes, the artist applied a watercolor wash and began painting the final images—usually starting with the farthest point in the background and working up to the foreground.

Offset Printing and Binding: Ringier America, New Berlin, Wisconsin
Color Separations: Offset Separations Corporation, Turin, Italy
Composition: Trufont Typographers, Hicksville, New York
Production Manager: Karen Gillis
Designer: Marc Cheshire